AF576309

PROJECT MARS 2050 /

PROJEKT MARS 2050

Herstellung und Verlag:

BoD - Books on Demand, Norderstedt

ISBN 978-3-7534-3525-1

PROJECT MARS 2050

A science fiction story by WALTER HAIN

They start to the greatest journey in the history of mankind and they find the incredible.

English version page 5

Deutsche Version Seite 61

PROJECT MARS 2050

A science fiction story by WALTER HAIN

They start to the greatest journey in the history of mankind and they find the incredible.

JERUSALEM – 30 AD

The city which lies at the feet of the two Romans is filled with movement; nevertheless it seems as if deadly silent. The people in the streets hardly speak to each other; many walk about with lowered faces, as if they feel personally responsible for what has happened. A light breeze is blowing, and the clouds hang heavily over the city. In some intangible way, the atmosphere is spooky and threatening.

"Today will be the day," says the Roman. "Today they will crucify him." "Who?" asked the other one who stood next to him. “You know, the Nazarene,” replied the Roman. “Oh yes, since he arrived, strange things have happened. Many think he’s the Messiah.” “If he really is, he could have prevented all this,” the Roman ventured. “I don’t know, maybe he planned it all this way,” replied the other one. “Come on, let’s go up to the Mount of Judgement!’

The three crosses lay ready on the slope of the hill. In the middle, the cross of the Nazarene, to its left and right those of the fellow condemned. The last hammer blows echo across the roofs of the nearby houses. Then the crosses are tilted upright and anchored in the ground. The two condemned writhed in agony while the Nazarene did not utter a sound. He just silently looked at the two women who, in tears, stood below him. One of the condemned braced himself and addressed the Nazarene: “I know that you are someone special. If I could, I would go with you." The Nazarene lifted his head lightly, slowly moved his lips and spoke: "Even this day, you will be with me." The blood ran across his forehead, and from the wounds on his hands and feet. A woman screamed from the surrounding crowd: "What have they done!'

The bodies of the two condemned collapsed into themselves, and their weight cut deep wounds into the flesh. Blood streamed from the cuts. The Nazarene slowly moved his head and turned his gaze upwards. There, in the sky, a small star was glowing, even though it is only afternoon, and still relatively light. With his last remaining energy, he called out: "Father, you wanted it this way!" Then his body, too, sank into the nails on the cross.

The wind rose to a storm and became ever stronger. The people standing around had trouble standing their ground. The clouds were gathering threateningly, and it became darker and darker. In the middle of the clouds, the star continued to glow. It even seemed to have grown in size. "It is a sign!" someone in the crowd screamed. "It is him!" "Look!" called someone else. "The star!'

The star seemed to be getting closer and closer. It kept getting larger and brighter. It scintillated in all the colours of the rainbow, and rotated like a child's top. Something is there, inside it, but the brilliant glow is already blinding the bystanders. One is calling out: "It is a miracle!" while protecting his eyes with his hand. "Yes, it's a miracle," exclaimed another, and, blinded, turned aside. The light grew until it was almost unbearable, and then quickly faded until it finally vanished. The storm subsided, and a brooding silence settled on the scene. The bystanders kneeled and prayed.

2020 YEARS LATER IN A SMALL TOWN IN THE UNITED STATES

"Wake up, Mr. Parker! Wake up, Mr. Parker! Wake up, Mr. Parker!" A soft female voice is coming from the video-alarm. Parker pressed a button. "Good morning. Thank you for getting up!" the voice continued, and the small screen lit up. Parker switched on the video wall. "Here is the World News," a speaker announced. "Tensions in the Persian Gulf have escalated further. The United Nations have assembled in an emergency session. A trade boycott is being considered." Parker stretched, ran his hand through his hair and sat on the edge of the bed. The speaker continued: "The whole world is breathlessly waiting for the launch of the two Mars space ships. The greatest trip ever risked by man commences today. Magellan and Columbus would be amazed if they could witness this event. We have just been informed that the astronauts are already on their way to the control stations. We will be back with more shortly." A commercial followed. Parker yawned and switched off the flat screen. He went into the kitchen, where Sue Ann, his wife, was already working at the microwaves. George, their young son, is sitting at the table.

"Good morning!" Parker offered. "Good morning!" replied the other two. "Well, George, did you do your homework? You know that today is a big day. Your finals," he says to his ten-year old son, and stroked his hair. George, bored, replied: "I know, but that goes for you, too." "How right you are," said Parker, and kissed Sue Ann on the forehead. Parker sat down at the table, and Sue Ann followed him with the English tea to which he has become accustomed since his marriage to the English girl. They all eat in silence.

After a while, Parker glanced over his shoulder into the lounge room. There, on the book shelf, lay an old copy of a German book and some American books which he has often skimmed. He opened a book and looked at a picture in the book. "I don't know, I don't believe that this thing up there is an artefact," he says to Sue Ann. "But even our scientists have examined those Mars shots and came to the same conclusions. That face-shaped mountain in particular looks quite fantastic," says Sue Ann. "In that case, the evolution of man would have proceeded quite differently to the way we have always assumed," replied Parker. "That's what you lot are supposed to find out now," Sue Ann says almost teasingly, and moved over to caress Parker. "Despite the great importance of your mission, I hate to let you go, John," she sighed. "It will be OK!" Parker replied consolingly. "I'll be back for sure. George will look after you while I'm gone," he says with a glance at his son. "He's a dear boy."

“Are you taking Lucy with you?” George asked. “No, I can’t,” Parker replied. “We are not allowed to take animals with us.” “But such a tiny monkey hardly needs any room,” George pleaded, “and besides, Lucy wants to be famous one day, too.” “Sorry, it’s out of the question,” Parker says sternly, and looked at his watch. “Gosh, it’s time! I have to get to the control centre; please get my things ready, Sue Ann.” Parker went into the bedroom and got dressed. Several minutes later, he returned. Sue Ann and George were already standing there, in readiness. They knew what they were in for. It would be goodbye for a whole fifteen months, or maybe more – who could say with certainty? “Look after yourself, John,” Sue Ann says with moist eyes. “And you two! See you,” Parker replied, and hugged the two firmly. Outside, the taxi is already waiting to take him to the control station. Parker kissed his wife and his son one more time and left, carrying his luggage. He climbed into the taxi and drove off. Sue Ann and George waved.

Twenty years have passed since the leading heads and scientists of some states on Earth decided to build the two Mars space ships. Numerous cargo rockets and shuttles carried the components into Earth orbit. There, they have been assembled into the most gigantic space ships ever constructed by mankind.

One of the two ships, the Tsiolkovski, is a mighty ship built under Russian supervision in cooperation with Chinese scientists. The experiences gained with the Russian and American space stations proved invaluable. The crew, under Commander Andreij Malinov, consisted further of the Afghan Koulaghi, the Frenchman Julien Piccard und Malinov's wife Svetlana. The Afghan is an experienced doctor, and has successfully looked after the Russian cosmonauts for years. The Frenchman is rather an adventurer, pilot in the French air force and an outstanding mountain climber. He has already conquered two twenty-five thousand footers, solo. Svetlana Malinov would be responsible for navigation and, in an emergency, could also take over the controls. But all have been trained in multiple skills, and could take over one or other function of the other crew members.

John Parker would be the Commander of the other space ship, the Lowell; a space ship which is in every way the equal of the Tsiolkovski. Both space ships are in fact very similar in construction, so that in an emergency each could be controlled by either crew. But everyone hoped that this would not eventually have to be tested. The command unit of the Lowell, like that of the Tsiolkovski, is relatively spacious. Parker and the Scotsman David McCray would sit up front; McCray would be the navigator and, if necessary, could take over the controls. Chris Mulligan, the female biologist and doctor, would be next; and Jack Nichols, the Canadian, who is responsible for communications, would sit behind them. The four seats are comfortable and could be swung to the side; each rear seat has a little wall-table with a monitor. The front of the command unit has a large, divided, panoramic window and to the left and right of that are two further small windows.

Andreij Malinov, the commander of the Tsiolkovski, is a very different type from Parker. He has worked his way up in the military academy, and is a veteran with several space flights to his credit. Together with his wife Svetlana and the cosmonaut Yuri Tretlov, he has already spent several years in space stations. He is a somewhat sullen type who would rather have flown to Mars on his own, but even he could not get around the international regulations. Besides, there is a lot of prestige and money at stake, and the major powers all expect to get a piece of the action. Nevertheless, it was Russian space probes that were the first to land on Mars. The first space traveller is a Russian, and the first artificial satellite has been of Russian origin. But that did not mean that space belonged to the Russians.

The Americans have also been very successful in space travel. They were the first to land humans on the Moon. They had the first big space station. And finally, they discovered in the middle of the last century these strange structures on Mars.

But, since the Perestroika efforts of the Russians in the last century, there has also been more emphasis on cooperation in space travel with some countries, not only with the Americans. Andreij Malinov would still get his chance. The Russian scientists, too, had been studying the satellite pictures of those structures on Mars for years.

Two main control centres have been constructed for the Mars mission: one in Moscow and one in Houston, Texas. Various other data centres in Japan, China, India, Australia and Europe would follow the entire mission. An international television network has been installed. Each important detail of the events during the flight and on the ground at Mars is to be reported in various presentations involving international star personalities. The entire transmission would extend over fifteen months. Between the news from the mission and local events on Earth, historical portrayals and old films about Mars would be shown. A never before attempted media event, of gigantic, global dimensions, is ready to unfold.

When Parker arrived at the Houston control centre, he met a frantic hive of activity. Even before he entered, the journalists were swarming around him with their incessant questions, and there were also a few shady types with their posters protesting against the mission. The posters carried sentiments such as STOP THE MARS FLIGHT, UNNECESSARY WASTE OF PUBLIC FUNDS and similar messages. Religious fanatics waxed enthusiastic in word wars. Somebody rambled something about the truth of the Bible; another one yelled: "Down with the Christians!" Too many rumours have been generated in recent years. Perhaps for that reason, it is time for the mission to clarify the situation.

The rockets in Baikonur and at Cape Canaveral which would take the four crew members of each of the space ships into Earth orbit are standing in readiness. The presidents of the United States and the

Russian Federation each made speeches with appropriate words wishing the travellers all the best with the success of the mission. Then the two took off simultaneously, in perfect launches from opposite sides of the world. The rockets flew directly to their space ships: the Russian one to Tsiolkovski, the American one to Lowell. The crews transferred and took up their stations. Then everything was checked out once more, with the aid of the ground station. Several hours later, the two Mars ships took off from their orbits amid great celebrations and cheering in the control stations. They soon reached the escape velocity which would start them on their way to Mars.

From the point of the crews, the blue Earth is shrinking steadily. The two space ships have already crossed the Moon's orbit. The Earth is no longer as "tangibly" close as it has been for the Moon astronauts in those distant days. The crews of the Mars ships are soon on their own. Soon no one would be able to help them. Direct assistance from Earth is no longer possible. The regular radio contact with the control station would be the only link with Earth for about fifteen months.

"Hello, Commander Parker, how are you? Is everything OK?" says the voice, in broken English, issuing from the loudspeaker of the Lowell's command unit. It is immediately evident that it is Parker who replies, in not less broken Russian: "Good, thank you, Malinov! Everything here is satisfactory!" The monitors flickered, and the indicator panels flashed. Malinov confirmed that his crew in the Tsiolkovski, too, are well. The routine tasks in both space ships proceeded apace; in about six months they would arrive at Mars. One of the first nights approached.

LOWELL
NASA
USS
W. Hain '91

“Chris and I will get a bit of shut-eye: you take over in the meantime, David. In six hours, we’ll relieve you,” Parker said. Chris went ahead, and Parker followed her into the airlock. The biologist is very attractive. Her looks are a delight to any man. The tight suit is stretched over her slim figure, and her blonde tresses fall, silky and shiny, across her shoulders. She is also very intelligent, and not approachable to every man. But Parker has not been able to hide, for some time, that he is keeping an eye on her. She swings through the door into the airlock. Parker follows her and closes the door behind him.

All units accessible to the crew have been constructed from cylindrical rocket units. They are fitted together with spherical airlocks. The airlock to the command unit is connected via the airlock to the logistics module, the habitation module and two others. These two units are arrayed one behind the other; they contain scientific apparatus and instruments on both sides, and through the centre there is a long passage which leads to the hygiene stations and the sleeping compartments module. In these modules oxygen is available everywhere, so that the crew do not need to put on space suits in order to get from one unit to the other. Only on the other side of the hygiene station and the sleep compartment is this part of the space ship connected by long, grid-like aluminium trusses to the rest of the ship. That is where the lander unit is, along with the instrumentation unit and the propulsion module. To get there, one has to climb into a space suit. A state of near zero gravity prevails on the whole ship, since the Mars ships are unable to generate their own gravity. For this reason, Parker and the biologist more or less floated down the passage between the two units arrayed on each side, towards the hygiene stations and sleep compartments. These are accessible via an airlock through which the two first have to pass.

"I'll just go and freshen up a bit," Chris says. "OK," Parker replies. "I want to get a few things from the sleep compartment." The biologist enters the hygiene station. The room is fitted with two showers, two wash-basins and a toilet. Various cupboards for toiletry articles and towels have been fitted to the walls. Chris undresses and climbs into one the showers. "Thank you for taking a shower," a soft voice says. "You may use six cubic litres of water. please hurry." The rationing is necessary, although the waste water is regenerated in a filter system. The biologist climbed out of the shower. "I don't know whether I'll be able to get used to that," she thought, and dried herself with a large towel. She wrapped herself in the towel and blow-dried her hair, which she then combed conscientiously. Some minutes later, she left the room and opened the door to the sleeping quarters.

The sleeping module is of the same size as all the other units. On both sides, two bunks are recessed into each wall. In the middle, there is a door which divided the unit into two smaller rooms, giving each room two bunks. The bunks can be closed off by means of a dark tinted plastic panel, providing somewhat of a private space for each occupant. The beds are quite comfortable, and well padded. Various wall cupboards have been provided.

As Chris entered the sleeping quarter, she saw Parker moving back and forth, looking for something. "It must be somewhere here," he said and rummaged around in his luggage. "I hear it clearly," he continued. "What did you hear?" Chris asked. "Squeak!" "That's what!" Parker exclaimed. "It must be come from one of the trunks." "Squeak!" "Damn, where IS that thing?" Parker muttered. "It must be this one," he shouted and opened one of the trunks. A little something looked at him with large, shiny eyes. "Squeak!'

"That prankster!" Parker burst out. "So he really smuggled Lucy into my luggage! Or did she get in there by accident?" "My God, but it's cute!" Chris exclaimed when she saw the tiny monkey. "It's name is Lucy, and it's my boy's," Parker said. "He was trying to persuade me to take her with me before I left. Naturally, I refused. But now we're stuck!" "But it's so cute," Chris says, and carefully took the tiny monkey in her hands and stroked it. "Well, we can't do anything about it now," Parker says, resigned. "But we have to look around for a cage of some sort, so that she doesn't get lost. And we'll have to share some of our food with her," he continued. "Some of our leftover food!" Chris corrected him. "Well, I suppose," says Parker. "With your consent, and if you look after it." "Of course!" Chris says immediately.

"But first of all, we should give her something to eat; she looks quite exhausted." "I'll see what I can find," Parker said, and went back to the habitation module. After a short time, he returned with a piece of bread and some fruit which the monkey devoured greedily. "I think she will be best accommodated in the habitation module; it will be the least trouble there," Parker says. "But for today, we can leave her here." Parker punched a few holes into one of the trunks which had seen better days, and laid the little monkey inside it. "Good night, Lucy, you'll be the first monkey on Mars," Chris says. "Near Mars," Parker corrected. "Because we won't be able to take her with us in the landing module." "Oh, well, that's something, anyway," Chris said thoughtfully, and leaned against Parker. "When do we arrive there, anyway?" she asked. "Soon, honey," he said tenderly, and they kissed. They lay down on the bunks and slept towards a new day.

McCray, the Scotsman yelled out, laughing: “Ha, ha, I won!” It is one of the following evenings in the habitation module, and they are playing “Catch the Martians,” a board game which they have come to enjoy back on Earth. One of them takes on the part of the Martians, and the others have to win as many tokens as possible from him. Several drinking containers with fruit juice and drinking tubes are fitted to the table. Finally the Canadian put the dice and tokens away. He and David were once again on night duty. Chris stood up and said: “I’m going to bed, I’m bushed!” Parker says: “I’ve still got something to deal with in the command module; I’ll be there soon.”

After a while, Jack says: “I’ll see how Parker’s doing.” “OK,” says the Scotsman. The Canadian slunk down the passage of the two longitudinal units and entered the airlock leading to the hygiene unit. He heard the faint splash of water. "She must be in the shower," he thought. He swung, almost noiselessly, into the bathroom, and quickly shut the door behind him. The biologist is standing in front of one of the hand-basins in her bath-robe, combing her hair. Jack leapt upon her; she screamed. "Help!" He threw her on the floor and tried to force his way between her thighs. She yelled again, and resisted with all her strength. "Now I've got you baby!" the Canadian exclaimed with an excited voice. "Now you're mine!" "Help! Help! John!" Chris screamed, while the Canadian tried to cover her mouth with his hand. She bit, hard. "Ouch! You bitch!" he yelled, and his lust seemed to have no end. The biologist defended herself as best she could. The two collided with the wall, the shower, and then rolled on the floor. "Help! Help," Chris screamed, full of desperation. Someone grabbed the Canadian by the shoulder. "You dog!" Parker shouted, and caught the Canadian with a right hook to the face. Jack collapsed into the shower compartment; the water switched on and streamed over him. "Thank you for taking a shower. You may use...," sounds a voice.

"Are you all right? What happened?" Parker asked. "Yes, yes, I'm OK," Chris replied and fell into his arms. "That bastard, he must have gone crazy!" she says. "Don't worry," Parker says, and with an angry look, turned to the Canadian. "You'll live to regret this, boy! You're endangering the entire mission! I'm going to make a report about you in the log book, you know that." The Canadian wiped his mouth with the back of his hand and stood up. "I'm sorry. But..." "No buts!" Parker replied. "We discussed such eventualities often enough, in the sex seminar; you should know what's involved here!" "That's all very well for you, with your...," replied Jack. Parker interrupted him. "Chris is chosen after extensive and difficult tests, and she has the same opportunities as all the other applicants. So get a grip on yourself in future. I do not want to see a recurrence of this!" The Canadian withdrew.

The days passed and became weeks. Mars gradually became visible as a small red disk. Already, the first features could be made out. The gigantic Valles Marineris canyon system is soon clearly discernible, and then the two huge volcanic cones in the Tharsis region. The two crews commenced the manoeuvres which would get them into an orbit. "Up to now, everything has gone like clockwork," Malinov says to Svetlana. "We'll see what awaits us on Mars." The intention is to land in the vicinity of the Mars pyramid and the "face" rock, in the Cydonia region. One lander unit from each ship, each with two crew members, is to make a landing there.

Parker and the biologist are assigned to "night

duty'; the Scotsman and the Canadian are fast asleep. Parker looked out of the porthole. Earth is now visible only as a small star. The sun is mirrored in the external panels of the Lowell's modules. It is a tranquil, almost majestic sight. Countless stars are twinkling. "Fantastic!" Chris breathed, and stared out of the window. "Yes...," Parker replied, "it's really romantic." She cuddled up to him and kissed him. Parker took her in his arms and returned her kiss. She sat on his lap; both embraced passionately. Parker could feel Chris's soft contours through her tight suit. He opened the zipper of her suit and put his hand inside. He stroked her breasts. She moaned: "Not here!" "Where else?" Parker rejoined. "Come on, I'll switch the autopilot on," he said, stood up and went over to lock the door. She was silent.

Parker turned on a music video. Somebody sang the Golden Oldie "Unchained Melody." They stood up and went over to the middle of the room, between the chairs. They danced slowly. Then they embraced closely and kissed passionately. Chris put her tongue wildly into Parker's mouth and raced it around inside; he knows that he is a dog, but then again he has to survive for fifteen months away from his wife; but they would be fifteen months with Chris. "Oh, I need your love...," the loudspeaker went on.

The two spaceships have reached Mars; they steer into orbit around the planet. The red planet is right under their feet. "Get ready to land," says Parker's voice through the loudspeakers.

It is evening over the landing area. The sun throws long shadows across the plain as the two lander units approach the Martian surface. "This face… it's incredible!" the Frenchman exclaimed, amazed. "It really looks like… no... or maybe yes…?" From one moment to the next, the rock seemed to change in the weak rays of the dying sunlight. Perhaps those who think it's a representation of Christ are correct; or perhaps those who see the Indian god Hanuman in the rock. In any event, it is a puzzlingly human face, which somehow has a prehistoric air about it. "We're going down," Parker says. "Malinov, how are things over there?" he asked the Russian. "Excellent, we can land," the latter replied. A short time later, Malinov's voice echoed through the space ships, the lander units and – much later – through the control centres on Earth: "Birdie has landed!" This is followed by general celebrations. Once again, the Russians have been first! Only a few minutes later, Parker also lands his module on the Martian surface; once again, there is enthusiastic applause all around.

The two landers have landed within only a few miles of each other. The astronauts have to put in a rest period. They all need a few hours" sleep. The night descends like a black veil over the Cydonia region, as though the god of war is intent on hiding his mysteries one last time. They all sleep deeply and peacefully.

The next day broke; the little sun rose in the East and once again threw long shadows across the plain. The sky is painted in hues varying from pale red to yellow. A brisk breeze is blowing. It brushes past the cylindrical landing modules and raised eddies of dust. The astronauts could almost imagine that they were back on Earth; the weightlessness is considerably less than it has been in the spaceships. Parker is making himself a cup of tea; the Canadian is also awake. Malinov and the Frenchman, in the other lander module, are already having breakfast.

"A very good Martian morning to you!" Parker's

voice is heard in both landing modules. The other replies, as in a chorus: Goo… d mor… ning!" A video flickered into life in each lander. "Hey, boys! We hope you have a nice day," one of the mission controllers at the control centre in Houston is heard to say. Two other video screens flickered: "S dobrym utrom!" is the greeting from a speaker in Moscow. "Prepare for checklist procedure!" the voice from Houston comes back. Both crews test all instruments for functionality. After a while, both commanders reported: "All in order!" OK, boys, let's go!" Houston replied.

The astronauts climbed, through an opening in the middle, into the lower compartment of their lander modules. This part of each module contains a vehicle not unlike the one that has already been used on Earth's Moon a long time earlier. They put on their space suits and then they open a great flap on the outside of the landers, which also served as ramps. They climbed into the vehicles and activated the batteries. With a short jolt, they moved forward and slowly glided down the ramp. The wind is still quite brisk, and visibility is not very good. "Everything in order?" Parker enquired via the headphones in the helmets. "All OK!" is the general consensus; which also signifies that the communication systems are functioning.

The Mars vehicles drove on, and simultaneously transmitted the scene via the data stations to television screens around the Earth. The pictures on Earth didn't show the real-time events, since the transmission – because of the vast distance – incurred some minutes delay. That has been the greatest hurdle in the control of the earlier automatic Mars vehicles. This time, the astronauts would be able to instantly adapt to every eventuality on site. But the television pictures are of far better quality than the pictures of the first landings on the Moon and Mars. Parker and the Canadian drove their vehicle toward the square pyramid mountain; Malinov and the Frenchman headed for the face-like mountain.

From the ground, the face-like mountain hardly looked like a human face; but of course, the view isn't so good from this angle. But one eye socket is visible as a huge hollow. As the two astronauts approached, the nose-shaped peak of the mountain and the split of what is identified as the mouth came into view. "Perhaps the best view is intended to be had from a height?" the Frenchman mused. "But for whom?" he continued. The mountain stretched out for the best part of about one and a half to two miles, with a height of about eight hundred feet. It was an awe-inspiring sight.

The vehicle came to a halt at the foot of the mountain, and the two astronauts prepared for the ascent. They have both gone through a comprehensive training course in mountain climbing. The Frenchman is a specialist in this field. He has conducted the appropriate training sessions on Earth. In mountain climber circles, he is an acknowledged leading light. The two hitched themselves to a rope, and Julien led the way.

They climbed up the projection which, in the

view from above, corresponded to the hairline. It stretched nearly across the entire length of the mountain. So far, there were no distinctly manmade features discernible in this massive rock. The two worked their way toward the eye socket. When they arrived there, gasping with the exertion, the Frenchman peered down into the huge cavity and jerked backwards. He put his hand protectively across his face. Something was blinding him. The entire depression had an estimated width of about sixty feet. In the middle, a cupola-shaped structure arched upwards, partly covered by the red sand, and glistening in the sunlight. It appeared to be made of a different material from the rock. A seam ran right across the dome; or at least something that looked like a seam. "What does it mean?" Malinov asked the Frenchman. "I don't know," the Frenchman replied.

The two continue climbing up, toward the tip of the nose. When they arrive much further up, they see that the other eye socket, too, contains a dome-shaped mound. “It’s a really spooky sight,” says Malinov. Suddenly, Parker’s voice is heard, shouting, in the helmets of both: “Julien, Malinov; can you hear me? Come over here immediately! It’s an emergency!” “What’s up?” the Russian asks. “It’s something … something’s happened to Jack… please come here immediately!” Parker screamed. The Frenchman and the Russian hurried down.

What had happened?

Parker and the Canadian had climbed some five hundred metres up the four-sided, pyramid-shaped mountain. It looked as though it consisted of four gigantic walls. The total width of the mountain was about one kilometre. This gave an almost square interior of about the height of the mountain. When the two arrived at the peak and looked over the escarpment, the interior revealed itself as a huge shaft that seemed to have no end. Despite this, the two astronauts braved a descent into the interior. The Canadian clipped himself to a rope whose end Parker fastened into the ground with a pulley. As well as that, the American grabbed the rope with both hands.

In this way, Jack climbed gradually deeper and deeper. Often pushing himself off the sides with his feet, he descended into the deep, almost playfully. "I don't know if Houston would have given us permission for this," Parker says. "I just want to see how far down this goes," the Canadian replied. "Besides, climbing expeditions, at our discretion, are intended to be part of the programme," Jack continued. "Be careful, anyway," Parker says. Suddenly, the Canadian cried out; the rope flashed through Parker's hands and zoomed through the pulley with lightning speed. It was all that the American could do to grab the rope with his remaining strength, but it dragged him to the very edge of the abyss. He braced his feet against it, slid, and came to a stop at the edge. Now he was screaming into the microphone as loud as he could, and the Canadian was dangling, unconscious, on the other end of the rope.

And now Parker is screaming into the microphone in a powerful voice and the Canadian dangles unconscious from the rope.

Malinov and Julien arrived at the pyramid mountain. They climbed up. When they arrived at the top, the American was still standing at the edge, as if rooted to the ground, desperately grasping the rope which is already digging into the gloves of his space suit. "Hurry up, I can't hold it any longer!" Parker screamed. "Did you want to get rid of him?" the Frenchman asked, referring to the incident in the space ship. "Don't be ridiculous!" Parker replied.

"Come and help me!" The Frenchman fastened the rope on the pulley, and Parker sank to the ground, exhausted.

"I will climb down," Julien said, anchoring his pulley in the rock. He descended hastily, following the Canadian's rope. This created a large degree of friction at the edge of the abyss, across which the rope descended. "He should have got the Russian to hold the rope," Julien was just thinking, when the rope broke with a mighty jolt. The Frenchman cried out as he started to plunge into the black nothingness. He collided with the Canadian, who was still unconscious. Julien instinctively flung out his hands, and at the last moment was able to grab the Canadian's rope. Now they are both hanging on the one rope, and it is only due to a miracle that it has not broken or been ripped out of its anchorage; even though the jolt would have been three times as severe on Earth.

When the Frenchman had recovered somewhat, he immediately recognised that his only chance was for him to pull himself and the Canadian up together. He fastened himself to the Canadian's rope with his carbine hook, and with the utmost exertion dragged the Canadian and himself up, centimetre after centimetre. "I hope the rope holds," Julien thought. The minutes passed, each one seeming like an eternity to the Frenchman. They had made it more than halfway. Suddenly, there was another powerful jerk. "Damn! Shiiiit...," the Frenchman screamed as they both plummeted into the depths of the gigantic shaft. With vigorous movements, the Frenchman sought something to grab onto. The Martian sky, and with it the whole shaft, started to spin like some kind of crazy carousel, while the opening became ever smaller and more distant. The Frenchman blacked out, too; a springy movement arrested their fall.

After a few minutes the Frenchman heard someone say: "Hey, partner! Wake up!" The Canadian must have regained consciousness somehow. "What's up? Where are we?" Julien asked. "I haven't got a clue either," Jack replied. "I just wondered when I woke up in this horrid stuff." The Frenchman looked around. He couldn't see much, since it was nearly totally dark. He looked up. The square mouth of the shaft seems from here to be only a few feet tall. The Martian sky above it provided only a weak light. Julien fumbled with his space suit and pressed a button. His helmet lamp flashed on and almost blinded him. "Thank God it's working!" he thought. The Canadian tried his luck, too, and was also successful. They both looked around. The movements of their heads and the changing light of the helmet lamps created an eerie scene. Somehow, everything around them looked as though it was damp. The rock walls were glistening.

Both are lying like flies in a gigantic net which also seems to be saturated with moisture. Fragments are already hanging off the mesh of this strange structure, and small rips are noticeable. The net is stretched across the entire width of the shaft. It feels like rubber, but seems to be much harder. In any case, it has saved the two astronauts from certain death; because to all appearances, the shaft continues down much further, and sooner or later they would have hit the rocky bottom – or whatever is down there.

"Julien! Jack! What's happened to you two? Are you still alive?" Parker's voice resounded in both their helmets. "Yes, so far everything is OK!" Julien replied. "We landed in a strange net! Perhaps it is intended as a safeguard against falling stones? Somebody must have installed it here!" says Julien. "It's good to hear your voices!" says Parker. "But you are too far down, and we haven't got another rope to come and help you; we will go to the lander module and get another one! We've also got a rescue basket there!" "Just a moment!" the Canadian cried out. "I can see something!" A square aperture is visible on one wall of the shaft. "There's a passage or something here," Jack says. "We'll have a look and report back!" "OK!" Parker replied. "It could be a chance to get out of there; but be careful!'

Julien and Jack worked their way across the rubbery net and over to the opening in the wall with rocking movements. The Canadian is the first to swing himself into the opening. "It really is a long passage!" he shouted. "And there… there's a light over there! It could be a way out." "Good, let's try it," the Frenchman, who had meanwhile also entered the passage, added. "Hello, Parker, we've found a passage here, which looks like it might lead to the outside!" Julien reported. "OK, check it out!" the American replied. "In the meantime, I will wait here in case you have to come back. Malinov will go by himself to get a new rope and the rescue basket. If you find an exit, call me!'

The two astronauts slowly worked their way down the passage. "Look at that," the Frenchman exclaimed. "What sort of symbols are these?" There are strange written symbols at regular intervals on the walls. "Evidently aids to orientation," Julien remarked. "Could be," the Canadian countered, "but we have to keep going, the exit is already nearer; the light is getting stronger. Our oxygen won't last much longer." "Maybe we can come back later and get a few shots of these signs," Julien said. "I don't think I'll be coming back this way," the Canadian ventured.

Julien was the first to arrive at the end of the

passage and, shocked, yelled: "That's incredible! It's fantastic! I have never seen anything like this in my life!" The Canadian joined him; they were both overcome by the sight which presented itself to them. Instead of the exit they had expected, they are confronted by an enormous cathedral fashioned in glistening rock and ice. It sparkled and flashed like a glass fairytale castle. Gigantic icicles are attached to the floor, the walls and the ceiling. "Where's that light coming from?" the Canadian asked. "It looks somehow phosphorescent," was the Frenchman's opinion. "Look, Julien, down there!" Jack shouted. On the ground, in the middle of the enormous ice dome, lay two grey slabs with a cylindrical table between them. "Come on, we have to check that out!" Julien shouted, and they both climbed down.

Past icy boulders, they finally arrive at one of the slabs. It is totally smooth and does not seem to be made of stone. There are no markings or anything of the sort on the slab. “Look, Julien!” the Canadian suddenly exclaimed and pointed to the top end of the slab. “It could be a type of sarcophagus.” A fine seam ran all the way around the slab, almost as though it could be fitted with a lid. “Come on, Jack!” the Frenchman said. “Help me slide this thing.” They both pushed hard with their hands against what they thought might be a lid. It was easier than they expected. With a sudden lurch, the slab opened almost halfway. At the same instant, air rushed into its interior and both shrank back... “That’s unbelievable! Look at this, Jack!” the Frenchman cried out. He was just able to make out a human-like form before it collapsed into a skeleton in the same instant.

It is a human skeleton, but a little larger than that of an average human. It seems to be a good two metres tall and the skull is covered with long, white hair. The hands, like human hands, have five fingers. The arms are stretched out and crossed over the loin; the entire skeleton is lying on its back. “How long has it been lying here, I wonder?” Julien says questioningly and with a glance at the Canadian. “Is it human or…?’

“I don’t dare open the second slab,” the Frenchman says. “Who knows what we might destroy there.” “But what are those strange markings on the cylinder?” Jack says. “Just a minute!” the Frenchman replied, as they both slowly walked towards the cylindrical table. “There are six symbols,” Julien said and shouted: “Yes, of course!” “That’s the ancient Egyptian ankh symbol, also called the ankh key; and that’s a Mayan glyph. This here is the sign of the Buddha, the Buddha cross, which is also known as the fylfot or swastika. Here we have the half-Moon and the five-pointed star, the symbols of Islam, and here the six-pointed Jewish star, or star of David; and here you can see the Latin passion cross, the Christ symbol. They are all religious symbols!" the Frenchman concluded. "And here in the middle, look, Julien, this truncated pyramid inside a circle!" Jack says. "Yes, that must be significant," Julien replied and continued: "But what?" "Is it maybe supposed to mean that all religions have a common source?" the Canadian asked. "And the key to that lies here on Mars!" the Frenchman continued. "Possible?" Jack says. "But then whose body is it in the slab?" Julien pressed on. "Is it David, Moses, Buddha, Mohammed, one of the Mayan gods or even Jesus?" "I don't know!" the Canadian answered.

They both walked around the cylinder. "Really strange that these symbols are here," Julien says, immersed in thought and absent-mindedly touching the Star of David. Suddenly, the entire ice palace resounded to the lamentation songs of countless Jews: "Ah, ah, eeh... !" "Incredible!" the Frenchman exclaimed. They both looked up into the gigantic ice dome and turned to all sides. "And what about this one?" Jack asked, touching the Mayan symbol. The sound of drums and songs of the original inhabitants of America mixed with the lamentation songs of the Jews: "Ah, ah, eeh, ehja, tom, tom...!" "And this one?" the Canadian says and touched the half-Moon. The prayer songs of the muezzins mixed with the lamentation songs, the Indian drums and songs: "Ah, ah, eeh, ehja, tom, tom, alah...!

"Fantastic!" Julien cried out and touched the Buddha sign. Indian sitars became audible, and Chinese harps, in addition to the other sounds. Then the Frenchman pressed the ankh symbol and Egyptian priests sang their songs of dead. And finally, when he pressed the cross of Christ, Byzantine chants and

Gregorian choirs by monks and organ sounds are added to the din: "Ah, ah, eeh, ehja, tom, tom, alah, uhh, teng, hooo…! Ah, ah, eeh, ehja …!" The whole thing rose to an ear-shattering choral crescendo. The entire ice dome roared under the sounds. The two astronauts tried to cover their ears with their hands, but the helmets prevented that. "Ah, ah, eeh, ehja ...!'

"Press the knob in the middle!" the Frenchman yelled. Jack's hand slammed down on the pyramid-shaped object in the centre of the cylinder. "Ratatatata…!" Machine gun salvos mixed with the religious din; rifle shots were added; revolvers and pistols rang out; bombs and grenades exploded; people screamed in horror. "Ah, ah … ehja ... ratatatata, boom..." Sirens wailed. It was a terrifying, infernal din, which kept on getting louder and louder. The entire ice cathedral shook under the noise. The two astronauts spun as if tormented by pain, and instinctively holding their hands protectively in front of their helmets, turned in all directions. The racket could not be stopped. The entire thing rose into an infernal scene of roaring and raging in all colours of the spectrum of sounds, tones and songs.

Suddenly, a crashing sound! A huge icicle crashed to the ground at the feet of the two astronauts. They ducked and jumped aside. Again, an immense crash! The next icicle landed with a crash. Then another, and again another. A stupendous crackling and snapping penetrated the entire room; one crash followed the other; the entire ice dome seemed to be ready to collapse. Fear gripped the two astronauts. The Frenchman screamed: “We’ve got to get out of here!” The Canadian probably didn’t even hear him. They both ran, scrambled, and slid towards the exit from which they have arrived. No other exit was apparent.

And still the infernal din continued. Gasping, they climbed into the opening. The Frenchman looked around. A great icicle fell down and hit the pyramid-shaped knob in the middle of the cylindrical table. Suddenly the din stopped. Only here and there, a muted crackle was audible. Then all was deathly silence. The walls of the gigantic ice palace glistened as they had before, almost as though nothing had happened; only now the place looked like the aftermath of a battle of the ice giants. The two slabs and the cylindrical table in the middle of the room are covered with numerous ice fragments. The lid of one slab lay on the ground, the other remained unopened.

"Come on, we have to leave!" the Frenchman says. "Our oxygen supply is nearly exhausted. The only chance we've got is to retrace our steps along the passage. Hopefully, Parker is at the shaft. Maybe he can help us to get out there now?" "OK, let's go!" the

Canadian replied. The two sought the shaft, a little more in a hurry than before.

When they arrived at the shaft, the Frenchman looked up. There was no trace of Malinov or Parker. Julien tried to activate the radio in his space suit. He shouted into the microphone: "Hello Parker! Hello Malinov! Can you hear us? Are you up there?" There is no answer. The Frenchman tries again: "Hello Parker! Hello Malinov! Can you hear us?" Suddenly, there is a crackle in the headphones in his helmet. "Where the hell have you been, are you OK?" Parker's voice is heard. Relieved, the Frenchman replies: "We're back here again! We didn't find an exit! Only something absolutely fantastic…! But can you haul us up?" "Of course!" Parker countered. "We've done a bit of pottering around here, and we've rigged up a device for you that we can use to get you up." "Great!" the Frenchman says. "We're lowering a rescue basket for you!" Parker finished.

Malinov and Parker hauled the two others up over the edge of the shaft. The Frenchman and the Canadian fell to the ground, exhausted. "My God, you should have seen it…!" Julien said, gasping, and shook his head. "It's unbelievable… this huge ice palace… and then those slabs… but we'll tell you about it later." "Yes!" Parker replied. "We have to get back to the lander modules now. It's time to fly home. Malinov and I have collected a few soil samples." "In my pocket there..." the Frenchman replied. "I've got… a lump of ice from the cave… there seem to be micro-organisms enclosed in it." "Yes, yes, let's look at it when we're back in the space ship!" Parker said. The four astronauts climbed into the two vehicles and drove towards the lander units.

The launches of the two lander modules are flawless and almost simultaneous. The Mars dust which had been stirred up settled back and restored the view of the surroundings. It was a somewhat sad view, although they were all pleased to be leaving. The lander units described a long arc over the square pyramid and the face rock. The crews of the landing units, lost in thought, look again across the Cydonia plain. “There! Something is moving!” the Frenchman exclaimed excitedly. They all looked down. The two dome-shaped objects in the eye cavities of the face-shaped mountain have opened up. Something shimmering, glistening, emerges. As with shining eyes, the strange mountain seems to look at the astronauts one last time.

Or would they meet again?

The situation on Earth has changed. It is not like before when they started.

The story continues – someday!

PROJEKT MARS 2050

Eine wissenschaftliche Erzählung von

WALTER HAIN

Sie starten zur größten Reise in der Geschichte der Menschheit und sie finden das Unfassbare.

JERUSALEM – 30 NACH CHRISTUS

In der Stadt, die den beiden Römern zu Füßen liegt, herrscht reges Treiben; dennoch wirkt sie wie totenstill. Die Menschen in den Gassen sprechen kaum miteinander; viele gehen mit gesenkten Häuptern aneinander vorbei, so als fühlen sie sich schuldig an dem, was geschehen war. Ein leichter Wind weht und die Wolken hängen schwer über der Stadt. Es ist irgendwie eine gespenstisch, bedrohliche Atmosphäre. „Heute wird es so weit sein", sagt ein

Römer. „Heute werden sie ihn kreuzigen.“ „Wen?“, fragt der andere Römer, der neben ihm steht. „Na, den Nazarener“, sagt der erste Römer. „Ach ja, seit der hier ist, haben sich merkwürdige Dinge ereignet. Viele halten ihn für den Messias.“ „Wenn er das wirklich ist, hätte er doch das alles hier verhindern können“, meint der zweite Römer. „Ich weiß nicht, vielleicht hat er das selbst so gewollt“, erwidert der erste. „Komm, lass uns auf den Gerichtsberg gehen!“

Drei Kreuze liegen bereit auf der Anhöhe des Berges. In der Mitte das des Nazareners, links und rechts davon die der beiden mit ihm Verurteilten. Die letzten Nagelschläge hallen über die Dächer der angrenzenden Häuser. Dann werden die Kreuze aufgerichtet und im Boden verankert. Die beiden Verurteilten winden sich in Schmerzen, während der Nazarener keinen Laut von sich gibt. Er blickte nur stumm zu den beiden Frauen, die weinend unter ihm stehen. Einer der Verurteilten fasst sich und spricht zu dem Nazarener: „Ich weiß, dass du etwas Besonderes bist. Wenn ich könnte, würde ich mit dir gehen.“ Der Nazarener hebt leicht den Kopf, bewegt langsam die Lippen und spricht: „Noch heute wirst du mit mir sein.“ Das Blut rinnt ihm über die Stirn und von den Wunden an den Händen und Füßen herab. Eine Frau ruft aus der umstehenden Menge: „Was haben sie nur getan!“

Die Körper der beiden Verurteilten sacken nacheinander in sich zusammen und ihr Gewicht schneidet tiefe Wunden in das Fleisch. Blut strömt erneut aus den Wunden. Der Nazarener bewegt langsam den Kopf und blickt nach oben. Dort leuchtet ein kleiner Stern, obwohl es erst Nachmittag ist und noch relativ hell. Mit letzter Kraft ruft er: „Mein Vater, du hast es so gewollt!“ Dann sinkt auch sein Körper in die Nägel am Kreuz.

Der Wind hebt sich zu einem Sturm und wird immer heftiger. Die umstehenden Leute haben Mühe, sich am Boden zu halten. Die Wolken ziehen sich bedrohlich zusammen und es wird immer dunkler. Inmitten der Wolken leuchtet noch immer der Stern. Ja, er scheint jetzt größer geworden zu sein. „Es ist ein Zeichen!“, schreit einer aus der Menge. „Er ist es gewesen!“ „Da seht nur!“, ruft ein anderer. „Der Stern!“

Der Stern scheint immer näher zu kommen. Er wird immer größer und heller. Er schillert in allen Farben und dreht sich wie ein Kreisel. Irgendetwas ist darin zu sehen, doch die Helligkeit blendet bereits die umstehenden Leute. Einer ruft noch: „Es ist ein Wunder!“, während er sich schützend die Hand vor die Augen hält. „Ja, es ist ein Wunder!“, ruft ein anderer und wendet sich geblendet ab. Das Licht steigert sich fast unerträglich, bis es schließlich verschwindet. Der Sturm legt sich und es herrscht wieder bedrückende Stille. Die umstehenden Leute knien nieder und beten.

2020 JAHRE SPÄTER IN EINER KLEINSTADT IN DEN VEREINIGTEN STAATEN

„Wachen Sie auf, Mr Parker! Wachen Sie auf, Mr Parker! Wachen Sie auf, Mr Parker!“, tönt eine sanfte weibliche Stimme aus dem Videowecker. Parker drückt auf einen Knopf. „Guten Morgen! Danke, dass Sie aufgestanden sind!“, ergänzt die Stimme und der kleine Bildschirm schaltet sich ein. Parker schaltet den Flachbildfernseher an der Wand ein. „Wir bringen nun die Weltnachrichten“, meldet ein Sprecher. „Die Spannungen am Persischen Golf haben sich weiter verschärft. Die Vereinten Nationen sind zu einer Krisensitzung zusammengetreten. Es wird ein Handelsboykott in Erwägung gezogen.“ Parker streckt sich, fährt sich durch die Haare und setzt sich auf die Bettkante. Der Sprecher setzt fort: „Die ganze Welt wartet gespannt auf den Start der beiden Marsraumschiffe. Die größte Reise, die je von Menschen gewagt wurde, wird heute beginnen. Magellan und Kolumbus würden erblassen, wenn sie das sehen könnten. Wie wir gerade erfahren haben, sind die Astronauten bereits munter auf dem Weg zu den Kontrollstationen. Wir werden uns in Kürze wieder melden." Ein Werbespot folgt. Parker gähnt und schaltet den Bildschirm aus. Er geht in die Küche, wo bereits seine Frau Sue Ann am Mikrowellenherd hantiert und sein Sohn George am Tisch sitzt.

„Guten Morgen!", sagt Parker. „Guten Morgen!", erwidern die beiden. „Na, George, hast du deine Hausaufgaben gemacht? Du weißt ja, heute ist ein großer Tag für dich. Es sind Abschlussprüfungen", sagt er zu seinem zehnjährigen Sohn und streicht ihm übers Haar. George erwidert gelangweilt: „Ich weiß, aber das gilt auch für dich.“ „Wie du recht hast“, sagt Parker und küsst Sue Ann auf die Stirn. Parker setzt sich an den Tisch und Sue Ann folgt ihm mit dem englischen Tee, den er sich seit der Heirat mit der Engländerin angewöhnt hat. Alle essen schweigend.

Nach einer Weile blickt Parker über seine Schulter ins Wohnzimmer. Dort liegen im Bücherschrank eine alte Kopie eines deutschen Buches und einige andere amerikanische Bücher, die er schon öfters durchgeblättert hat. Er öffnet ein Buch und sieht sich ein Bild in dem Buch an. „Ich weiß nicht, ich glaube nicht, dass dieses Ding da oben künstlich ist“, sagt er zu Sue Ann. „Aber auch unsere Wissenschaftler haben die Marsaufnahmen untersucht und sie kamen zu denselben Vermutungen. Besonders dieser gesichtsförmige Berg sieht sehr erstaunlich aus“, meint Sue Ann. „Dann wäre die Entwicklung der Menschheit ganz anders verlaufen, als wir bisher angenommen haben“, erwidert Parker. „Das sollt ihr ja nun herausfinden“, meint Sue Ann fast neckisch und schmiegt sich an ihren Mann. „Trotz dieser weitreichenden Bedeutung eurer Mission lass ich dich nicht gerne gehen, John“, seufzt sie. „Es wird schon gut gehen“, meint Parker tröstend. „Ich komme bestimmt zurück. George wird einstweilen auf dich aufpassen“, sagt er mit einem Blick zu seinem Sohn. „Er ist ja ein lieber Junge.“

„Nimmst du Lucy mit?“, fragt George. „Nein, das geht nicht!“, erwidert Parker. „Wir dürfen keine Tiere mitnehmen.“ „Aber so ein kleines Äffchen wie Lucy braucht doch nur wenig Raum“, sagt George bittend. „Es will auch einmal berühmt werden.“ „Es tut mir leid, es geht nicht!“, erwidert Parker streng und schaut auf seine Armbanduhr. „Mensch, es ist Zeit! Ich muss zum Kontrollzentrum; mach bitte meine Sachen fertig, Sue Ann." Parker geht ins Schlafzimmer und zieht sich an. Nach einigen Minuten kommt er zurück. Sue Ann und George stehen schon bereit. Sie wissen, was auf sie zukommen wird. Es wird ein Abschied für ganze fünfzehn Monate sein oder vielleicht auch mehr; wer kann das schon mit Bestimmtheit sagen. „Pass auf dich auf, John!", sagt Sue Ann mit feuchten Augen. „Ihr auch auf euch! Ich komme bestimmt wieder. Macht's gut", erwidert Parker und drückt die beiden fest an sich. Draußen wartet schon das Taxi von der Kontrollstation. Parker küsst seine Frau und seinen Sohn nochmals und geht mit dem Gepäck hinaus. Er steigt ins Taxi und fährt ab. Sue Ann und George winken.

Zwanzig Jahre sind vergangen, seit die führenden Staatsoberhäupter und Wissenschaftler beschlossen hatten, die beiden Marsraumschiffe zu bauen.

Zahlreiche Transportraketen und Shuttles hatten die Einzelteile in eine Erdumlaufbahn gebracht. Dort wurden sie dann zu den gigantischesten Raumschiffen, die je von Menschen konstruiert wurden, zusammengebaut.

Eines davon, die Ziolkowski, ist ein mächtiges Schiff, das unter russischer Leitung gebaut wurde. Die Erfahrungen mit den früheren russischen und amerikanischen Raumstationen konnten dabei voll genutzt werden. Die Besatzung unter dem Kommandanten Andreij Malinow wird weiters aus dem Afghanen Koulaghi, dem Franzosen Julien Piccard und Malinows Frau Svetlana bestehen. Der Afghane ist ein erfahrener Arzt und betreute bereits jahrelang erfolgreich die russischen Kosmonauten. Der Franzose ist eher ein Abenteurer, Flieger der französischen Luftwaffe und ein ausgezeichneter Bergsteiger. Er hat bereits zwei Achttausender im

Alleingang geschafft. Svetlana Malinow wird für die Navigation zuständig sein und notfalls kann sie auch die Steuerung des Raumschiffes übernehmen. Alle sind vielseitig ausgebildet und können die eine oder die andere Tätigkeit jedes Besatzungsmitglieds übernehmen.

John Parker wird der Kommandant des anderen Raumschiffs sein, der Lowell; ein Raumschiff, das der Ziolkowski um nichts unterlegen ist. Beide Raumschiffe wurden nämlich sehr ähnlich konstruiert, sodass jedes im Notfall von einer der beiden Besatzungen gesteuert werden kann. Doch es hofft wohl keiner, dass das jemals der Fall sein würde. Die Kommandoeinheit der Lowell ist, wie die der Ziolkowski, relativ geräumig ausgestattet. Vorne werden Parker und der Schotte David McCray sitzen; dieser wird als Navigator fungieren und kann ebenfalls die Steuerung des Raumschiffs notfalls übernehmen. Dahinter wird die Biologin Chris Mulligan sitzen und hinter ihr Jack Nichols, der Kanadier, der für die Kommunikation zuständig ist. Die vier Sitze sind bequem und können zur Seite geschwenkt werden; jeder Rücksitz hat einen kleinen Wandtisch mit Monitor. Die Vorderseite der Kommandoeinheit hat ein großes geteiltes Panoramafenster und links und rechts davon zwei weitere kleine Fenster.

Andreij Malinow, der Kommandant der Ziolkowski, ist ein ganz anderer Typ als Parker. Er hat sich in der Militärakademie hochgearbeitet und bereits etliche Raumflüge hinter sich. Gemeinsam mit dem Kosmonauten Juri Tretlow und seiner Frau Svetlana verbrachte er bereits mehrere Jahre in Raumstationen. Er ist ein eher mürrischer Typ, der lieber alleine zum Mars geflogen wäre, doch die internationalen Bestimmungen konnte auch er nicht umgehen.

Außerdem liegt in dieser Mission viel Prestige und viel Geld auf dem Spiel, von dem sich die Großmächte einiges erwarten. Dennoch waren es sowjetische Raumsonden, die erstmals auf dem Mars niedergingen. Der erste Raumfahrer war ein Russe und auch der erste künstliche Erdsatellit stammte von den Russen. Der Weltraum gehört aber deswegen nicht den Russen.

Die Amerikaner waren auch sehr erfolgreich in der Raumfahrt. Sie waren die Ersten, die mit Menschen auf dem Mond landeten. Und sie hatten die erste große Raumstation. Und schließlich entdeckten sie in der Mitte des vorigen Jahrhunderts diese merkwürdigen Gebilde auf dem Mars.

Aber seit den Perestroika-Bemühungen im vorigen Jahrhundert legt man auch in der Raumfahrt mehr Gewicht auf Zusammenarbeit mit mehreren

Ländern, nicht nur mit den Amerikanern. Andreij Malinow wird aber seine Chance noch bekommen. Auch die russischen Wissenschaftler studieren schon seit Jahren die Satellitenaufnahmen von diesen merkwürdigen Gebilden auf dem Mars.

Für die Marsmission wurden zwei Hauptkontrollzentren eingerichtet: eines in Moskau und eines in Houston. Verschiedene andere Datenzentren in Japan, China, Indien, Australien und Europa werden die gesamte Mission verfolgen. Ein internationales Nachrichtennetz wurde eingerichtet. In verschiedenen Showblöcken mit internationalen Stars wird über jede wichtige Einzelheit während des Fluges und des Aufenthalts auf dem Mars berichtet. Über fünfzehn Monate hindurch wird sich die gesamte Berichterstattung erstrecken. Zwischen den Meldungen von der Mission und den lokalen Ereignissen auf der Erde werden geschichtliche

Darstellungen und Filmdokumentationen über den Mars gesendet. Ein noch nie dagewesenes Medienereignis von gigantischem globalem Ausmaß kann beginnen.

So trifft Parker im Kontrollzentrum in Houston auf eine entsprechende Hektik. Schon vor dem Eingang überfallen ihn die Journalisten mit zahlreichen Fragen. Es gibt auch einige zwielichtige Typen mit Transparenten, die gegen die Mission protestieren. STOPPT DEN MARSFLUG, UNNÖTIGE VERSCHWENDUNG VON STAATSGELDERN und Ähnliches war darauf zu lesen. Religiöse Fanatiker erhitzen sich in Wortgefechten. Irgendjemand faselt etwas von der Wahrheit der Bibel; ein anderer schreit: „Nieder mit den Christen!“ Zu viele Gerüchte sind in den letzten Jahren in Umlauf gebracht worden. Vielleicht sollte auch deshalb mit diesem Unternehmen Klarheit geschaffen werden.

Die Raumfährenraketen in Baikonur und Cape Canaveral, die die jeweils vier Besatzungsmitglieder der Marsraumschiffe in eine Erdumlaufbahn bringen werden, stehen dampfend auf ihren Starttürmen bereit. Die Staatspräsidenten der USA und Russlands halten Ansprachen und wünschen den Astronauten alles Gute zum Gelingen der Mission. Dann erfolgen gleichzeitig die beiden Starts, die perfekt gelingen. Die Raketen fliegen direkt zu ihren Raumschiffen; die russische zur Ziolkowski, die amerikanische zur Lowell. Die Besatzungen steigen um und nehmen ihre Plätze ein. Dann wird mit Hilfe der Bodenstationen nochmal alles durchgecheckt. Einige Stunden später starten die beiden Marsraumschiffe aus den Umlaufbahnen unter großem Jubel und Beifall in den Kontrollzentren. Sie erreichen die Fluchtgeschwindigkeit, die sie in Richtung Mars bringen wird.

Die blaue Erde wird aus Sicht der Besatzungsmitglieder immer kleiner. Die beiden Raumschiffe kreuzen die Mondbahn. Die Erde wird nun nicht mehr so „greifbar“ nahe sein wie seinerzeit für die Mondastronauten. Die Besatzungen der Marsschiffe sind bald auf sich alleine gestellt. Bald kann ihnen niemand mehr helfen. Die Schwierigkeiten der Mission werden sie selbst bewältigen müssen. Eine Hilfe von der Erde aus ist nicht mehr direkt möglich. Der regelmäßige Funkkontakt mit den Kontrollstationen wird über fünfzehn Monate hindurch das einzige „Bindeglied“ zur Erde sein.

„Hallo, Kommandant Parker, wie geht es Ihnen? Ist bei euch alles in Ordnung?“, klingt es in gebrochenem Englisch aus dem Lautsprecher in der Kommandoeinheit der Lowell. Es ist sofort klar, dass es Malinow ist, der sich meldet. Parker erwidert in einem nicht weniger gebrochenen Russisch: „Danke, gut, Malinow! Alles läuft bei uns zufriedenstellend!“

Die Bildschirme flimmern und die Anzeigeboards blinken. Malinow bestätigt über Funk ebenfalls das Wohlbefinden der Mannschaft in der Ziolkowski. Die Routinearbeiten in beiden Raumschiffen gehen flott voran. In etwa sechs Monaten werden sie beim Mars sein. Eine der ersten Nächte bricht an.

„Chris und ich legen uns aufs Ohr; übernimm du einstweilen, David. In sechs Stunden lösen wir euch ab“, sagt Parker. Chris geht voraus und Parker folgt ihr in die Schleuse. Die Biologin ist sehr attraktiv. Ihr Anblick ist eine Augenweide für jeden Mann. Der enge Anzug spannt sich um ihre schlanke Figur und das blonde Haar fällt seidig glänzend über ihre Schultern. Sie ist aber auch sehr intelligent und lässt nicht jeden Mann an sich heran. Parker kann es aber längst nicht mehr verbergen, dass er ein Auge auf sie geworfen hat. Sie schwingt sich durch die Tür in die Schleuse. Parker folgt ihr und schließt die Tür hinter sich.

Alle Einheiten, die von der Mannschaft betreten werden können, sind aus zylindrischen Raketeneinheiten angefertigt worden. Sie wurden mit kugelförmigen Schleusen aneinandergefügt. Die Schleuse zur Kommandoeinheit ist mit der Vorratseinheit, der Aufenthaltseinheit und mit zwei weiteren Einheiten verbunden. Diese zwei Einheiten sind hintereinander angeordnet; sie enthalten an beiden Seiten wissenschaftliche Apparate und Instrumente und durch die Mitte läuft ein langer Gang, der zur Sanitäreinheit und zur Schlafeinheit führt. In diesen Räumen ist überall Sauerstoff vorhanden, sodass niemand von der Besatzung einen Raumanzug anlegen muss, um von einer zur anderen Einheit zu gelangen. Erst nach den Sanitär- und Schlafeinheiten ist das Raumschiff durch lange gitterartige Aluminiumträger mit dem übrigen Ende des Schiffes verbunden. Dort befinden sich die Landeeinheit, die Geräteeinheit und das Antriebsaggregat. Will man dorthin gelangen, muss ein Raumanzug angelegt werden. In allen Räumen herrscht praktisch Schwerelosigkeit, da die Marsraumschiffe kein eigenes Gravitationsfeld erzeugen können. Überall an den Wänden sind jedoch zahlreiche Griffe angebracht, die das Fortbewegen erleichtern. Parker und die Biologin schweben also mehr oder weniger durch den Gang der beiden längsseits angeordneten Einheiten der Schlafeinheit und der Sanitäreinheit entgegen. Diese sind wieder mit einer Schleuse verbunden, durch die die beiden zuerst hindurchmüssen.

„Ich werde mich noch etwas frischmachen“, sagt Chris. „Okay!“, erwidert Parker. „Ich suche mir noch einige Sachen in der Schlafeinheit zusammen.“ Die Biologin betritt den Sanitärraum. Dieser ist mit zwei

Duschen, zwei Waschbecken und einer Toilette ausgestattet. An den Wänden sind verschiedene Schränke für Toilettenartikel und Handtücher angebracht. Chris zieht sich aus und steigt in eine der Duschen. „Danke, dass Sie sich duschen!“, sagt eine sanfte Stimme. „Sie haben sechs Kubikliter Wasser zur Verfügung. Bitte beeilen Sie sich.“ Die Rationierung ist notwendig, obwohl das Abwasser in einer Filteranlage regeneriert wird. Die Biologin verlässt die Dusche. „Danke, dass Sie geduscht haben! Auf Wiedersehen!“, sagt die Stimme. „Ich weiß nicht, ob ich mich an das gewöhnen werde“, denkt Chris und trocknet sich mit einem großen Badetuch ab. Sie hüllt sich in das Tuch und trocknet mit einem Föhn ihre Haare, die sie danach sorgfältig kämmt. Sie verlässt nach einigen Minuten den Raum und öffnet die Tür zur Schlafeinheit.

Die Schlafeinheit ist ebenso groß wie alle

anderen Einheiten. Je zwei Kojen sind links und rechts in die Wände eingelassen. In der Mitte befindet sich eine Tür, die die Einheit in zwei kleine Räume teilt; jeder Raum hat also zwei Kojen. Die Kojen können mit einer dunkel getönten Kunststoffglasscheibe geschlossen werden, sodass die Privatsphäre für jeden einigermaßen gewährleistet ist. Die Liegen sind recht bequem und gut gepolstert. An den Wänden befinden sich verschiedene Schränke.

Als Chris den Schlafraum betritt, sieht sie Parker suchend hin und her gehen. „Irgendwo muss es sein“, sagt er und kramt in seinem Gepäck herum. „Ich habe es doch deutlich gehört“, ergänzt er. „Was hast du gehört?“, fragt Chris. „Quiek!“ „Das da!“, sagt Parker. „Es muss aus einem der Koffer kommen.“ „Quiek!“ „Verdammt, wo IST das Ding?“, sagt Parker. „Dieser muss es sein!“, ruft er und öffnet einen Koffer. Ein kleines Etwas blickte ihn mit großen Augen an.

„Quiek!“

„Dieser Schlingel!“, ruft Parker. „Hat er doch tatsächlich Lucy in mein Gepäck geschmuggelt! Oder ist sie versehentlich hineingekommen?“ „Mein Gott, ist das süß!“, ruft Chris, als sie das kleine Äffchen sieht. „Es ist Lucy und sie ist von meinem Jungen“, sagt Parker. „Er meinte vor meiner Abreise irgendetwas vom Mitnehmen. Ich habe es natürlich abgelehnt. Jetzt haben wir die Bescherung!“ „Aber es ist doch lieb“, meint Chris und nimmt vorsichtig das kleine Äffchen in ihre Hände und streichelt es. „Nun, wir können jetzt nichts anderes dagegen tun“, sagt Parker resignierend. „Aber wir müssen uns nach einem Käfig umsehen, damit es nicht verloren geht. Und wir müssen einen Teil unseres Essens mit ihm teilen“, fährt er fort. „Einige unserer Essensreste“, korrigiert Chris. „Nun, ich nehme an“, sagt Parker, „mit deinem Einverständnis und wenn du dich darum kümmerst.“ „Natürlich!“, sagt Chris sofort.

„Aber zuerst sollten wir ihm etwas Essbares geben; es sieht ziemlich erschöpft aus.“ „Ich werde mal sehen, ob ich etwas finde“, sagt Parker und geht zur Aufenthaltseinheit zurück. Nach kurzer Zeit kommt er mit etwas Brot und Obst zurück, das der Affe gierig verschlingt. „Ich denke, es wäre am besten im Wohnmodul untergebracht; dort wird es am wenigsten lästig sein“, sagt Parker. „Aber für heute können wir es hier lassen.“ Parker schlägt einige Löcher in einen der Koffer, den er für nicht mehr ganz brauchbar hält und legt den kleinen Affen hinein. „Gute Nacht, Lucy, du bist das erste Äffchen auf dem Mars“, sagt Chris. „Beim Mars“, korrigiert Parker. „Denn wir können es sicher nicht mit dem Landemodul mitnehmen.“ „Na ja, das ist ja auch etwas“, sagt Chris und lehnt sich an Parker. „Wann werden wir eigentlich dort sein?“, fragt sie. „Bald,

Kleines“, sagt Parker zärtlich und sie küssen sich. Sie legen sich in die Kojen und schlafen einem neuen Tag entgegen.

McCray, der Schotte, ruft lachend: „Haha, gewonnen!“ Es ist an einem der folgenden Abende in der Aufenthaltseinheit und sie spielen Catch the Martians, ein Brettspiel, das sie schon auf der Erde liebten. Einer spielt die Rolle der Marsianer und die anderen müssen ihm möglichst viele Figuren abnehmen. Einige Becher Fruchtsaft mit Saugröhrchen sind am Tisch angebracht. Schließlich räumt der Kanadier die Würfel und die Figuren weg. Er und David haben wieder einmal Nachtdienst. Chris steht auf und sagt: „Ich gehe ins Bett, ich bin müde.“ Parker sagt: „Ich muss noch etwas in der Kommandoeinheit erledigen; ich komme gleich nach.“

Nach einer Weile meint Jack: „Ich sehe mal nach

Parker." „Okay!", sagt der Schotte. Der Kanadier schleicht durch den Gang der beiden längsseitigen Einheiten und betritt die Schleuse zum Sanitärraum. Dort hört er ein feines Plätschern von Wasser. „Sie muss in der Dusche sein", denkt er. Er schwingt sich fast lautlos in den Waschraum und schließt blitzschnell die Tür hinter sich. Die Biologin steht im Bademantel vor einem der Waschbecken und richtet sich die Haare. Jack stürzt sich auf sie; sie schreit auf. „Hilfe!" Er wirft sie zu Boden und versucht, sich zwischen ihre Schenkel zu drängen. Sie stößt noch einen Schrei aus und wehrt sich mit allen Kräften. „Jetzt hab ich dich, Puppe!", sagt der Kanadier mit erregter Stimme. „Jetzt gehörst du mir!" „Hilfe! Hilfe! John!", schreit Chris, während der Kanadier versucht mit seiner Hand ihren Mund zu bedecken. Sie beißt ihn in die Hand. „Au! Du Katze!", ruft er und seine Gier scheint nicht enden zu wollen. Die Biologin wehrt sich, so gut sie kann. Die beiden schlagen gegen die Wand, gegen die Dusche und wälzten sich am Boden. „Hilfe! Hilfe!“, schreit Chris voller Verzweiflung. Jemand packt den Kanadier an der Schulter. „Du Hund!“, ruft Parker und knallt dem Kanadier einen rechten Haken ins Gesicht. Jack stürzt in die Duschkabine; das Wasser schaltete sich ein und strömt über ihn. „Danke, dass Sie sich duschen! Sie haben …“, tönt eine Stimme.

„Wie geht es dir? Ist alles in Ordnung?“, fragt Parker Chris. „Ja, ja, es geht“, erwiderte sie und fällt ihm in die Arme. „Dieses Ekel, der muss verrückt geworden sein!“, sagt sie. „Ist schon gut“, sagt Parker und wendet sich mit einem wütenden Blick zu dem Kanadier. „Das wird für dich Folgen haben, Junge! Du gefährdest die ganze Mission! Ich muss eine Eintragung ins Logbuch machen; das weißt du.“ Der Kanadier fährt sich mit dem Handrücken über den Mund und steht auf. „Es tut mir leid! Aber …“

„Nichts aber!“, erwidert Parker. „Wir haben im Sexualseminar immer wieder solche Situationen besprochen; du solltest wissen, auf was du dich hier einlässt.“ „Du hast es ja gut mit deiner …“, erwidert Jack. Parker unterbricht ihn. „Chris wurde nach langen, schweren Tests ausgewählt, und sie hatte die gleichen Chancen wie alle anderen Bewerber. Also reiß dich in Zukunft zusammen. Ich möchte einen solchen Vorfall nicht mehr erleben!“ Der Kanadier entfernte sich.

Die Tage vergehen und werden zu Wochen. Der Mars wird nach und nach als kleine rote Scheibe sichtbar. Schon zeichnen sich erste Landstriche ab. Das gewaltige Valles Marineris ist bald deutlich zu sehen, dann auch die riesigen Vulkankegel in der Tharsis-Region. Die beiden Besatzungen leiten die Manöver zum Einschwenken in eine Umlaufbahn ein. „Bis jetzt ist alles zufrieden verlaufen“, sagt Malinow zu Svetlana. „Wir werden sehen, was uns auf dem Mars erwartet.“ Es ist vorgesehen, in der Nähe der Marspyramide und des Gesichtsfelsens im Gebiet Cydonia zu landen. Je eine Landeeinheit mit zwei Leuten an Bord soll dort niedergehen.

Parker und die Biologin sind zur Nachtschicht eingeteilt; der Schotte und der Kanadier schlafen fest. Parker blickt aus dem Bordfenster. Die Erde ist nur noch als kleiner Stern zu sehen. Die Sonne spiegelt sich an den Außenwänden der einzelnen Module der Lowell. Es ist ein beruhigender fast majestätischer Anblick. Zahlreiche Sterne funkeln. „Toll!“, sagt Chris und schaut aus dem Fenster. „Ja …“, erwidert Parker, „es ist richtig romantisch.“ Sie lehnt sich an ihn und gibt ihm einen Kuss. Parker nimmt sie in die Arme und erwidert ihren Kuss. Sie setzt sich zu ihm auf seinen Schoß; beide umarmen sich leidenschaftlich. Parker fühlt durch den engen Anzug von Chris ihre weichen Formen. Er öffnet den Reißverschluss an ihrem Anzug und steckt seine Hand hinein. Er streichelt ihre Brüste. Sie stöhnt: „Doch nicht hier!“ „Wo sonst?“, erwidert Parker. „Komm, ich schalte die Automatiksteuerung ein“, sagt er und steht auf und verriegelt die Tür. Sie sagt nichts.

Parker schaltete ein Musikvideo ein. Einer singt den Oldie „Unchained Melody“. Beide stehen auf und stellen sich in die Mitte des Raumes zwischen die Stühle. Sie wiegen sich in langsamen Tanzschritten. Sie umarmen sich innig und küssen sich leidenschaftlich. Chris streckt ihre Zunge in Parkers Mund und fährt damit wie wild herum; er drückt seine Zunge gegen die ihre und beginnt damit zu spielen. Er muss an Sue Ann denken; er weiß, er ist ein Schweinehund, doch schließlich wird er fünfzehn Monate lang von ihr getrennt sein; aber das würden fünfzehn Monate mit Chris sein. „Oh, I need your love …“, tönt es aus dem Lautsprecher.

Die beiden Raumschiffe haben den Mars erreicht; sie steuern in eine Umlaufbahn um den Planeten. Der Rote Planet liegt direkt unter ihren Füßen. „Fertig machen zum Landen“, tönt die Stimme von Parker durch die Lautsprecher.

Es ist Abend über dem Landegebiet. Die Sonne wirft lange Schatten über die Ebene, als sich die beiden Landemodule der Marsoberfläche nähern. „Dieses Gesicht … Es ist unglaublich!“, ruft der Franzose erstaunt. „Es sieht tatsächlich aus wie … Nein … Oder doch …?“ Von einem Augenblick zum anderen scheint sich der Felsen im Schein des schwachen Sonnenlichts zu ändern. Vielleicht haben die einen recht, die meinen, das sei das Abbild Christi; oder vielleicht die anderen, die darin den indischen Gott Hanuman sehen. Es ist auf jeden Fall ein verblüffend menschliches Antlitz, das irgendwie prähistorisch wirkt. „Wir gehen runter“, sagt Parker. „Malinow, wie sieht’s bei Ihnen aus?“, fragt er den Russen. „Ausgezeichnet, wir können landen“, erwidert dieser. Kurze Zeit später ertönt die Stimme Malinows durch die Raumschiffe, die Landeeinheiten und – etwas später – durch die Kontrollzentren der Erde: „Vögelchen ist gelandet!“ Darauf folgt allgemeiner Jubel. Die Russen waren wieder einmal die Ersten! Nur wenige Minuten später setzt auch Parker mit seiner Landefähre auf dem Mars auf; auch darauf folgt allgemein großer Beifall.

Die beiden Lander sind nur einige hundert Meter voneinander entfernt. Die Raumfahrer müssen eine Ruhepause einlegen. Einige Stunden Schlaf haben alle nötig. Die Nacht senkt sich wie ein schwarzer Schleier über das Cydonia-Gebiet, als wolle der Kriegsgott noch ein letztes Mal sein Geheimnis bewahren. Alle schlafen fest und ruhig.

Der nächste Tag bricht an; die kleine Sonne geht im Osten auf und legt wieder lange Schatten über die Ebene. Der Himmel ist blassrot bis gelb. Es weht ein heftiger Wind, der an den zylinderförmigen Landeeinheiten entlangstreicht und einigen Staub aufwirbelt. Die Raumfahrer fühlen sich fast wie auf der Erde; die Schwerelosigkeit ist wesentlich geringer als in den Raumschiffen. Parker macht sich einen Tee; der Kanadier ist ebenfalls schon wach. Auch Malinow und der Franzose in der anderen Landeeinheit frühstücken bereits.

„Einen schönen guten marsianischen Morgen!“, ertönt Parkers Stimme durch die beiden Lander. Die anderen erwidern im Chor: „Gu…ten Mor…gen!“ Ein Bildschirm flackert in jeder Landeeinheit auf. „Hallo, Jungs! Wir wünschen euch einen schönen Tag“, sagt ein leitender Sprecher aus dem Kontrollzentrum in Houston. Zwei andere Bildschirme flackern. „S dobrym utrom!“, grüßt ein Sprecher aus Moskau. „Macht euch bereit, Leute, zum Durchchecken!“, ertönt wieder die Stimme aus Houston. Beide Besatzungen überprüfen alle Instrumente auf ihre Funktion. Nach einer Weile melden die beiden Kommandanten: „Alles bestens!“ „Okay, Jungs, dann macht euch auf die Socken!“, heißt es wieder aus Houston.

Die Raumfahrer steigen durch eine Öffnung in der Mitte in den unteren Teil ihrer Landeeinheiten. Dort befindet sich ein Fahrzeug, wie es ähnlich schon auf dem Erdmond benutzt wurde. Sie legen ihre Raumanzüge an und öffnen anschließend eine große Klappe an der Außenwand der Lander, die zugleich als Rampe dient. Sie steigen in die Fahrzeuge und starten die Batterien. Mit einem kurzen Ruck bewegen sie sich vorwärts und gleiten langsam die Rampe hinunter. Der Wind bläst noch immer recht heftig und die Sicht ist nicht sehr gut. „Alles in Ordnung?“, fragt Parker über die Kopfhörer in den Helmen. „Alles okay!“, ertönt es allgemein aus den Lautsprechern; was zugleich auch bedeutet, dass der Funkkontakt funktioniert.

Die Marsfahrzeuge fahren weiter und übermitteln gleichzeitig die Szenerie über die Datenstationen und Fernsehschirme der Erde. Die Bilder auf der Erde zeigen aber nicht die direkte Situation, da die Übertragung – aufgrund der großen Entfernung – mehrere Minuten dauert. Das war auch die größte Schwierigkeit beim Steuern der früheren automatischen Marsfahrzeuge. Diesmal können sich die Raumfahrer direkt vor Ort auf jede Situation sofort einstellen. Die Fernsehbilder sind aber von weitaus besserer Qualität als seinerzeit bei den ersten

Mond- und Marslandungen. Parker und der Kanadier fahren mit ihrem Fahrzeug zu dem quadratischen Pyramidenberg; Malinow und der Franzose zu dem Gesichtsfelsen.

Vom Boden aus sieht der Berg kaum wie ein menschliches Gesicht aus; aber die Sicht ist nicht so gut. Deutlich ist jedoch eine Augenhöhle als große Mulde zu erkennen. Als die beiden Raumfahrer näher kommen, zeigt sich auch die nasenförmige Spitze des Berges und die Spalte des Mundes. „Vielleicht ist der günstigere Anblick aus großer Höhe beabsichtigt?“, meint der Franzose. „Aber von wem?“, ergänzt er. Der Berg erstreckt sich über etwa zwei mal zweieinhalb Kilometer. Er hat eine Höhe von etwa zweihundertundvierzig Metern. Es ist ein gewaltiger Anblick.

Das Fahrzeug hält am Fuße des Berges und die

beiden Raumfahrer machen sich bereit zum Aufstieg. Beide haben eine umfangreiche Ausbildung im Bergsteigen hinter sich. Der Franzose ist darin Spezialist und er hat die entsprechende Ausbildung auf der Erde geleitet. Er ist in Bergsteigerkreisen eine anerkannte Kapazität. Die beiden hängen sich mit einem Seil zusammen und Julien beginnt mit dem Aufstieg.

Sie klettern den Vorsprung hinauf, der von oben aus dem Haaransatz des Felsengesichts entspricht. Er erstreckt sich fast über die ganze Länge des Berges. Es ist so weit nichts Künstliches an diesem Felsen zu erkennen. Die beiden gehen der Augenhöhle entgegen. Als sie dort keuchend ankommen, blickt der Franzose über die riesige Vertiefung und zuckt zurück. Er hält sich die Hand schützend vors Gesicht. Irgendetwas blendet ihn. Die gesamte Vertiefung ist schätzungsweise zweihundert Meter breit. In der Mitte wölbt sich ein kuppelförmiges Gebilde nach oben, das teilweise von rotem Sand bedeckt ist und das im Sonnenlicht glänzt. Es scheint aus einem anderen Material zu bestehen als das des Felsens. Quer über die Kuppel verläuft eine Naht; oder etwas Ähnliches. „Was hat das zu bedeuten?“, sagt Malinow zu dem Franzosen. „Ich weiß es nicht“, erwidert der Franzose.

Die beiden steigen weiter hinauf, der Nasenspitze zu. Als sie ziemlich weit oben angelangt sind, sehen sie auch in der zweiten Augenhöhle eine kuppelförmige Erhebung. „Es ist ein unheimlicher Anblick“, meint Malinow. Plötzlich kreischt Parkers Stimme durch die Helme der beiden: „Julien, Malinow; hört ihr mich? Ihr müsst sofort zu uns kommen! Es ist ein Notfall!“ „Was ist los?“, fragt der Russe. „Es ist etwas … etwas mit … Jack … kommt bitte sofort her!“, schreit Parker. Der Franzose und der Russe machen sich auf den Weg.

Was war geschehen?

Parker und der Kanadier waren die etwa fünfhundert Meter des viereckigen pyramidenförmigen Berges hinaufgeklettert. Er sieht aus, als bestünde er aus vier riesigen Mauern. Die gesamte Breite des Berges beläuft sich auf etwa einen Kilometer. Daraus resultiert ein fast quadratischer Innenteil, der etwa so breit ist wie die Höhe des Berges. Als die beiden am Gipfel ankamen und über die Böschung blickten, entpuppte sich dieser Innenteil als riesiger langer Schacht, der nicht zu enden schien. Dennoch wagten die beiden Raumfahrer einen Abstieg ins Innere. Der Kanadier hakte sich an einem Seil fest, dessen Ende Parker mit einer Rolle am Boden befestigte. Zusätzlich hielt der Amerikaner das Seil mit beiden Händen fest.

So stieg Jack nach und nach hinunter. Mit den

Füßen sich immer wieder abstoßend, ließ er sich fast spielerisch in die Tiefe hinab. „Ich weiß nicht, ob uns das Houston genehmigen würde“, meinte Parker. „Ich will ja nur sehen, wie weit es hier hinuntergeht“, erwiderte der Kanadier. „Außerdem sind ja Kletterpartien nach eigenem Ermessen im Programm vorgesehen“, ergänzte Jack. „Seien Sie auf jeden Fall vorsichtig“, sagte Parker. Plötzlich schrie der Kanadier auf; Parker glitt das Seil aus den Händen und es rollte sich blitzschnell ab. Der Amerikaner konnte es noch mit letzter Kraft fassen, doch es zerrte ihn zur Kante des Abgrunds. Er stemmte die Füße dagegen, rutschte und blieb kurz vor dem Abgrund stehen.

Und jetzt schreit Parker mit kräftiger Stimme ins Mikrofon und der Kanadier baumelt bewusstlos am Seil.

Malinow und Julien kommen beim

Pyramidenberg an. Sie klettern hinauf. Als sie oben ankommen, steht der Amerikaner noch immer wie angewurzelt vor dem Abgrund und hält krampfhaft das Seil fest, das sich schon in die Handschuhe seines Raumanzugs bohrt. „Beeilt euch, ich kann es nicht länger halten!“, schreit Parker. „Wolltest du ihn loswerden?“, fragt der Franzose und spielt dabei auf den Vorfall im Raumschiff an. „Ach was!“, erwidert Parker. „Hilf mir lieber!“ Der Franzose befestigt das Seil an der Rollenvorrichtung und Parker sinkt erschöpft zu Boden.

„Ich werde hinuntersteigen“, sagt Julien und verankert seine Rolle im Boden. Er lässt sich hastig am Seil des Kanadiers entlang hinunter. Dadurch entsteht eine heftige Reibung an der Kante des Abgrunds, über die das Seil läuft. „Er hätte dem Russen das Seil in die Hand geben sollen“, denkt sich gerade Julien, als dieses mit einem kräftigen Ruck reißt. Der Franzose stürzt mit einem Aufschrei in die Tiefe. Er prallt auf den Kanadier, der noch immer bewusstlos ist. Julien fährt instinktiv mit den Händen herum und kann noch in letzter Sekunde das Seil des Kanadiers fassen. Jetzt hängen beide an einem Seil und es ist wohl nur einem Wunder zu verdanken, dass dieses nicht gerissen oder aus der Verankerung gelaufen ist; obwohl der Aufprall auf der Erde dreimal stärker gewesen wäre.

Als sich der Franzose einigermaßen erholt hat, erkennt er sofort, dass ihm wohl nichts anderes übrig bleiben wird, als sich mit dem Kanadier gemeinsam hochzuziehen. Er hakt sich mit seinem Karabiner an dem Seil des Kanadiers fest und mit größter Anstrengung zieht er ihn und sich Zentimeter für Zentimeter nach oben. „Hoffentlich hält das Seil", denkt Julien. Minuten für Minuten vergehen, die dem Franzosen endlos scheinen. Die Hälfte der Strecke hat er bereits hinter sich. Plötzlich gibt es wieder einen kräftigen Ruck. „Verdammt! Scheißeee …!“, schreit der Franzose und beide stürzen in die Tiefe des riesigen Schachtes. Mit heftigen Bewegungen sucht der Franzose nach einem Halt. Der Marshimmel und mit ihm der ganze Schacht beginnen sich wie in einem gigantischen Karussell zu drehen, während sich die Öffnung immer mehr entfernt und kleiner wird. Der Franzose wird ebenfalls bewusstlos; eine federnde Bewegung fängt die beiden auf.

Nach einigen Minuten hört der Franzose jemanden sagen: „He, Kumpel! Wach auf!“ Der Kanadier muss irgendwie wach geworden sein. „Was ist los? Wo sind wir?“, fragt Julien. „Ich weiß es selbst nicht“, erwidert Jack. „Ich habe mich nur gewundert, als ich in diesem ekligen Zeug aufwachte.“ Der Franzose sieht sich um. Viel kann er nicht sehen, da es fast völlig dunkel ist. Er schaut nach oben. Die viereckige Öffnung des Schachtes scheint von hier aus nur einige Meter groß zu sein. Der Marshimmel darüber gibt nur ein schwaches Licht ab. Julien fummelt an seinem Raumanzug herum und drückt auf einen Knopf. Seine Helmlampe blitzt auf und blendet ihn fast. „Gott sei Dank funktioniert sie!“, denkt er. Der Kanadier versucht damit ebenfalls sein Glück und es gelingt auch ihm. Beide blicken sich um und durch die Kopfbewegungen und das wechselnde Licht der Helmlampen entsteht eine gespenstische Szene. Alles ringsherum wirkt irgendwie feucht und die Felswände glänzen.

Beide liegen wie Fliegen in einem riesigen Netz, das ebenfalls von Feuchtigkeit durchzogen scheint. Von den Maschen dieses merkwürdigen Gebildes hängen bereits Fetzen herunter und kleinere Risse sind zu sehen. Über die gesamte Breite des Schachtes ist dieses Netzwerk ausgespannt und es wirkt wie Gummi, doch scheint es wesentlich härter zu sein. Jedenfalls hat es die beiden Raumfahrer vor dem sicheren Tod gerettet; denn so wie es aussieht, führt der Schacht noch viel weiter hinunter und früher oder später wären sie auf dem Felsboden aufgeprallt – oder was immer da unten sein mag.

„Julien! Jack! Was ist los mit euch? Lebt ihr noch?“, ertönt die Stimme Parkers in den Helmen der beiden. „Ja, es ist so weit alles okay!“, erwidert Julien. „Wir sind hier von einem merkwürdigen Netz aufgefangen worden! Vielleicht ist es zum Schutz vor herabfallenden Steinen gedacht? Irgendjemand muss das hier installiert haben!“ „Es ist gut, eure Stimmen zu hören!“, sagt Parker. „Ihr seid aber zu weit unten und wir haben auch kein Seil mehr, um euch zu Hilfe zu kommen; wir werden zur Landeeinheit gehen und ein neues holen! Dort haben wir auch den

Rettungskorb!“ „Moment!“, ruft der Kanadier. „Ich sehe etwas!“ An einer Wand des Schachtes zeigt sich eine viereckige Öffnung. „Da ist irgendein Gang oder Ähnliches“, sagt Jack. „Wir sehen uns dort um und melden uns dann wieder!“ „Okay!“, ruft Parker. „Es könnte eine Chance sein, da rauszukommen; aber seid vorsichtig!“

Julien und Jack hanteln sich mit schaukelnden Bewegungen auf dem gummiartigen Netz zu der Öffnung in der Wand. Als Erster schwingt sich der Kanadier hinein. „Es ist tatsächlich ein langer Gang!“, ruft er. „Und da … dahinten ist ein Licht! Es könnte ein Ausgang sein.“ „Gut, dann versuchen wir es“, meint der Franzose, der mittlerweile ebenfalls den Gang betreten hat. „Hallo, Parker, wir haben hier einen Gang gefunden, der offenbar hinausführt!“, meldet sich Julien. „Okay, dann versucht es!“, erwidert der Amerikaner. „Ich werde hier einstweilen warten, falls ihr zurückkommen müsst. Malinow wird allein ein neues Seil und den Rettungskorb holen. Sollt ihr zu einem Ausgang kommen, meldet euch!“

Die beiden Raumfahrer gehen langsam den Gang entlang. „Da, sehen Sie!“, ruft der Franzose. „Was sind das für Zeichen?“ An den Wänden sind in regelmäßigen Abständen seltsame Schriftzeichen angebracht. „Offenbar sind das Orientierungshilfen“, bemerkt Julien. „Könnte sein“, erwidert der Kanadier, „aber wir müssen weiter, der Ausgang kommt schon näher; das Licht wird immer heller. Der Sauerstoff reicht ohnehin nicht mehr lange.“ „Vielleicht können wir später zurückkommen und noch einige Aufnahmen von diesen Zeichen machen“, meint Julien. „Ich glaube nicht, dass ich hier nochmal zurückkomme“, meint der Kanadier.

Julien kommt als Erster am Ende des Ganges an

und ruft erschrocken: „Das ist ja unglaublich! Das ist phantastisch! So etwas habe ich in meinem ganzen Leben noch nicht gesehen!“ Der Kanadier kommt zu ihm und beide sind überwältigt von dem Anblick, der sich ihnen bietet. Statt dem vermeintlichen Ausgang liegt eine riesige Kathedrale aus glänzendem Felsgestein und Eis vor ihnen. Es funkelt und glitzert wie in einem gläsernen Märchenschloss. Am Boden, an den Wänden und an der Decke ragen riesige Eiszapfen hervor. „Wo kommt dieses Licht her?“, fragt der Kanadier. „Es wirkt irgendwie phosphoreszierend“, meint der Franzose. „Sehen Sie, Julien, da unten!“, ruft Jack. Am Boden in der Mitte des gewaltigen Eisdoms liegen zwei graue Quader und dazwischen ein zylindrischer Tisch. „Kommen Sie, da müssen wir hin!“, ruft Julien und beide steigen hinab.

Über eisige Felsen hinweg kommen sie

schließlich an einem der Quader an. Er ist völlig glatt und scheint nicht aus Stein zu sein. Auf dem Quader befinden sich keine Schriftzeichen oder Ähnliches. „Sehen Sie, Julien!“, ruft plötzlich der Kanadier und deutet auf das obere Ende des Quaders. „Es könnte sich um eine Art Sarkophag handeln.“ Rings um den Quader läuft eine feine Naht, so als würde er einen Deckel haben. „Kommen Sie, Jack!“, sagt der Franzose. „Schieben Sie einmal mit an.“ Beide stemmen sich mit ihren Händen gegen diesen vermeintlichen Deckel. Es ist leichter, als sie gedacht haben. Mit einem plötzlichen Ruck öffnet sich der Quader fast bis zur Hälfte. Im selben Augenblick entsteht ein Luftsog ins Innere des Quaders und beide schrecken zurück. „Das ist ja ungeheuerlich! Sehen Sie, Jack!“, ruft der Franzose. Er kann gerade noch eine menschliche Gestalt ausmachen, als diese im selben Augenblick bis zum Skelett zerfällt.

Es ist ein menschliches Skelett, doch etwas

größer als von normalen Menschen. Es scheint gut zwei Meter groß zu sein und am Schädel trägt es langes, weißes Haar. Die Hände haben wie beim Menschen fünf Finger. Die Arme liegen ausgestreckt und gekreuzt über den Lenden; das gesamte Skelett liegt am Rücken. „Wie lange es wohl schon hier liegt?“, sagt Julien fragend und mit einem Blick zu dem Kanadier. „Ist es ein Mensch oder …?“

„Ich wage erst gar nicht den zweiten Quader zu öffnen“, sagt der Franzose. „Wer weiß, was wir damit noch zerstören.“ „Aber was sind das für seltsame Zeichen auf dem Zylinder?“, sagt Jack. „Warten Sie mal!“, erwidert der Franzose und beide gehen langsam zu dem zylindrischen Tisch. „Es sind sechs Symbole“, meint Julien und ruft: „Ja, natürlich!“ „Da ist das altägyptische Ankh-Zeichen oder auch Ankh-Schlüssel genannt und das da ist eine Maya-Glyphe. Hier, da ist das Zeichen des Buddha, das Buddha-

Kreuz oder auch Swastika genannt. Hier haben wir den Halbmond und den fünfzackigen Stern, das Symbol des Islam, und hier den sechszackigen Juden-Stern oder auch David-Stern; und hier sehen Sie das lateinische Passionskreuz, das Christus-Zeichen. Es sind alles religiöse Symbole!“, schließt der Franzose. „Und hier in der Mitte; sehen Sie, Julien, diese flache Pyramide innerhalb eines Kreises!“, sagt Jack. „Ja, das muss irgendeine Bedeutung haben“, erwidert Julien und setzt fort: „Aber was für eine?“ „Soll das vielleicht heißen, dass alle Religionen einen gemeinsamen Ursprung haben?“, fragt der Kanadier. „Und der Schlüssel dazu liegt hier auf dem Mars!“, ergänzt der Franzose. „Möglich?“, sagt Jack. „Aber wer ist dann dieser Tote in dem Quader?“, fragt Julien weiter. „Ist es David, Moses, Buddha, Mohammed, einer der Maya-Götter oder gar Jesus?“ „Ich weiß es nicht!“, meint der Kanadier.

Die beiden gehen um den Zylinder herum.

„Wirklich seltsam, dass diese Symbole hier sind", sagt Julien nachdenklich und tippt dabei unwillkürlich auf den David-Stern. Plötzlich hallt der ganze Eispalast unter den Klageliedern zahlloser Juden. „Ah, ah, eeh …!" „Unglaublich!", ruft der Franzose. Beide blicken hinauf in den riesigen Eisdom und wenden sich nach allen Seiten. „Und was ist mit dem da?", fragt Jack und tippt auf das Maya-Symbol. Es mischen sich Trommeln und Gesänge von den Ureinwohnern Amerikas unter die Klagelieder der Juden. „Ah, ah, eeh, ehja, tom, tom …!" „Und was ist hier?", sagt der Kanadier und tippt auf den Halbmond. Es mischen sich die Gebetsgesänge der Muezzins unter die Klagelieder und unter die Indianertrommeln und die Gesänge. „Ah, ah, eeh, ehja, tom, tom, alah …!"

„Phantastisch!", ruft Julien und tippt auf das Buddha-Zeichen. Es erklingen indische Sitars und chinesische Harfen zu den anderen Klängen. Dann drückt der Franzose das Ankh-Symbol und ägyptische Priester singen ihre Totenlieder; und schließlich kommen beim Drücken des Christus-Kreuzes noch byzantinische Gesänge und gregorianische Chöre von Mönchen und Orgelklänge dazu. „Ah, ah, eeh, ehja, tom, tom, alah, uhh, teng, hooo …! Ah, ah, eeha …! Das Ganze steigert sich zu einem ohrenbetäubenden Choral. Die ganze Eiskuppel dröhnt unter den Klängen. Die beiden Raumfahrer versuchen sich die Ohren mit den Händen zu bedecken, doch daran hindern sie ihre Schutzhelme. „Ah, ah, eeh, ehja …!“

„Drücken Sie auf den Knopf in der Mitte!“, schreit der Franzose. Jack knallt seine Handfläche auf das pyramidenförmige Gebilde in der Mitte des Zylinders. „Ratatatata …!“ Maschinengewehrsalven mischen sich unter den religiösen Lärm; Gewehrschüsse kommen hinzu; Revolver und Pistolen knallen; Bomben und Granaten explodieren;

Menschen schreien vor Entsetzen. „Ah, ah … ehja ... ratatatata, bumm …!“ Sirenen heulen. Es ist ein entsetzlicher, infernalischer Lärm, der immer lauter und lauter wird. Die ganze Eiskathedrale erbebt unter dem Lärm. Die beiden Raumfahrer drehen sich, wie von Schmerzen gepeinigt, instinktiv die Hände vor die Helme haltend, nach allen Seiten. Der Lärm ist nicht zu stoppen. Das Ganze steigert sich in ein infernalisches Szenarium von einem Brausen und Toben in allen Klangfarben, Tönen und Gesängen.

Plötzlich ein Krachen! Ein riesiger Eiszapfen stürzt zu Boden vor die Füße der beiden Raumfahrer. Sie ducken sich und springen zur Seite. Wieder ein Krachen! Der nächste Eiszapfen stürzt herab; dann wieder einer und wieder einer. Ein gewaltiges Knistern und Knacken durchdringt den ganzen Raum; ein Krachen folgt dem anderen; der ganze Eisdom scheint einzustürzen. Die beiden Raumfahrer packt die Angst. Der Franzose schreit: „Wir müssen da raus!“ Der Kanadier hat ihn wahrscheinlich gar nicht gehört. Beide rennen, klettern, rutschen dem Eingang zu, von dem sie gekommen sind. Kein anderer Ausweg scheint sich anzubieten.

Noch immer ertönt der infernalische Lärm. Keuchend klettern beide in die Öffnung. Der Franzose blickt sich um. Ein großer Eiszapfen fällt herab und trifft auf den pyramidenförmigen Knopf in der Mitte des zylindrischen Tisches. Plötzlich verstummt der Lärm. Nur hie und da ist noch ein Knacken zu hören. Schließlich wird es totenstill. Die Wände des riesigen Eispalastes glitzern wie zuvor, fast als ob nichts geschehen wäre; doch nun sieht es aus wie nach einer Schlacht von Eisriesen. Die beiden Quader und der zylindrische Tisch in der Mitte des Raumes sind von zahlreichen Eistrümmern bedeckt. Der Deckel des einen Quaders liegt am Boden, der andere bleibt ungeöffnet.

„Kommen Sie, wir müssen gehen!“, sagt der Franzose. „Unser Sauerstoffvorrat ist bald aufgebraucht. Es bleibt uns nur die Möglichkeit, den Gang wieder zurückzugehen. Hoffentlich ist Parker am Schachteingang! Vielleicht kann er uns inzwischen helfen da rauszukommen?“ „Gut, gehen wir!“, erwidert der Kanadier. Die beiden gehen, etwas eiliger als zuvor, dem Schacht entgegen.

Als sie beim Schacht ankommen, blickt der Franzose nach oben. Es ist keine Spur von Malinow oder Parker zu sehen. Julien versucht seinen Funk im Raumanzug zu betätigen. Er ruft ins Mikrofon: „Hallo, Parker! Hallo, Malinow! Hört ihr uns? Seid ihr da oben?“ Es kommt keine Antwort. Der Franzose versucht es nochmals. „Hallo, Parker! Hallo, Malinow! Könnt ihr uns hören?“ Plötzlich ein

Knacken im Kopfhörer seines Helms. „Wo steckt ihr denn, was ist los mit euch?“, ertönt Parkers Stimme. Erleichtert erwidert der Franzose: „Wir sind wieder hier! Wir haben keinen Ausgang gefunden! Nur etwas ganz Phantastisches …! Aber könnt ihr uns raufholen?“ „Klar!“, entgegnet Parker. „Wir haben ein wenig herumgebastelt und für euch eine Vorrichtung konstruiert, mit der wir euch hinaufziehen können.“ „Sehr gut!“, sagt der Franzose. „Wir lassen euch einen Rettungskorb hinunter!“, ergänzt Parker.

Malinow und Parker ziehen die beiden anderen über die Kante des Schachtes hinauf. Der Franzose und der Kanadier fallen erschöpft zu Boden. „Mein Gott, das hättet ihr sehen müssen …!“, sagt Julien keuchend und schüttelt den Kopf. „Es ist nicht zu glauben … dieser riesige Eispalast … und dann diese Quader … aber wir erzählen es euch später.“ „Ja!“, erwidert Parker. „Wir müssen jetzt zurück zu den

Landeeinheiten. Es ist Zeit, nach Hause zu fliegen. Ich habe mit Malinow einige Bodenproben gesammelt." „In meiner Tasche da …", erwidert der Franzose, „habe ich … einen Eisklumpen aus der Höhle … es scheinen Mikroorganismen darin eingeschlossen zu sein." „Ja, ja, das sehen wir uns dann im Raumschiff an!", sagt Parker. Die vier Raumfahrer steigen in die zwei Fahrzeuge und fahren den Landeeinheiten entgegen.

Die Starts der beiden Landemodule erfolgen ohne Probleme und fast gleichzeitig. Der aufgewirbelte Marsstaub senkt sich und gibt die Landschaft frei. Es ist ein etwas wehmütiger Anblick, obwohl alle froh sind, hier wegzukommen. Die Landeeinheiten schwenken in einem langen Bogen über die viereckige Pyramide und den Gesichtsfelsen. Die Besatzungen der Landeeinheiten blicken in Gedanken versunken noch einmal über die Cydonia-

Ebene. „Da! Es bewegt sich etwas!“, ruft der Franzose erregt. Alle blicken nach unten. Die beiden kuppelförmigen Gebilde in den Augenhöhlen des gesichtsförmigen Felsens öffnen sich. Irgendetwas Schimmerndes, Glitzerndes tritt hervor. Wie mit glänzenden Augen scheint der seltsame Berg die Raumfahrer ein letztes Mal anzublicken.

Oder werden sie ihn wiedersehen?

Die Situation auf der Erde hat sich geändert. Es ist nicht mehr so wie vor der Abreise der Raumfahrer.

Die Geschichte geht weiter … irgendwann!

This story is based on scientific discoveries from several Mars probes.

At first presented as PROJECT MARS 2020 by Walter Hain, Vienna, Austria in 1991

Registered from 1991 to 1998 in the Writers Guild of America

Thanks for translate at first in 1991 by Michael Krochmal. Ormond, Victoria, Australia